CHRISTMAS BONANZA

A TWISTED CHRISTMAS SHORT STORY

ALEXANDRIA BLAELOCK

BlueMere Books
MELBOURNE, AUSTRALIA

For permission requests, please contact
enquiries@bluemerebooks.com.

Ordering Information:
Discounts are available on quantity purchases. For details, contact orders@bluemerebooks.com.

Christmas Business/Alexandria Blaelock
paperback ISBN: 978-1-925749-99-1
digital ISBN: 978-1-922744-00-5

CHRISTMAS BONANZA

Edina was nervous.

It was September first; the day The Christmas Bo-nanza competition began.

It was the ultimate reality show; beauty, brains, and brawn. Open to men and women sixteen to twenty-six.

And of course, the ultimate winner deserves the ultimate prize.

The magnificent house and gardens were con-structed and furnished by the competitors. Brand new cars and clothes supplied by the sponsors.

And of course - a marriage made in heaven, be-tween the two fittest, smartest, most beautiful peo ple in the country.

With all that, it was no wonder The Christmas Bonanza was the most anticipated reality show on TV.

Competitors were voted off, back on, and off again by competitors and audience alike.

Challenges included hunting game and prepar-ing one or more meals for the other competitors.

Plus quizzes, talent shows, and survival skills. Winner takes all.

Edina sat on a Queen Anne style stool, facing herself in the triple mirrors of the dressing table, wondering if she was doing the right thing.

She picked up a photo of her family; Mum, Dad, four sisters and herself, the youngest.

She was young when it was taken, and it had seemed to her that anything was possible.

She was older now.

Cynical too.

Believed you had to work harder, not smarter, to get anywhere in life.

Was she was too old to win The Christmas Bo-nanza?

Too saggy, and bumpy, and daggy?

Too dumb?

It was worth it, right?

She desperately wanted to prove herself.

To her family, and to everyone who said she'd never amount to anything.

And this year was the last year she was eligible to enter; born on December 24th, she'd age out near the end of the competition.

Edina had resolved that this year, no matter the cost, she would do whatever it took.

She looked past herself, to the reflection of the room behind him.

The blue sponged walls looked like a warm summer sky. Deep blue wall-to-wall carpet, made you feel like you were lying on a tiny island in the middle of the Mediterranean as you lay in bed.

The Queen Anne bed, wardrobe, side and dressing tables she'd lovingly sanded back to the original birch and applied a clear stain.

The lacework doilies she'd made by hand to protect the furniture from her antique finds.

The watercolour beach landscapes she'd paint-ed and hung in white frames.

And the lush green indoor plants she threw away as soon as they got too big for the room.

On the whole, it presented a charming picture, one she was proud to leave the curtains open for passers-by to see just how beautiful it was.

Not a speck of dirt, or unplumped pillow, or carelessly thrown garment to mar its perfection.

That morning, however, the vine print curtains were closed.

She'd worked her butt off to prepare for the competition.

Training hard, she'd finally lost her puppy fat and built muscle. Her running times were the best they'd ever been.

She'd joined an academy, brushing up her edu-cation, and picking ikebana for her special knowledge.

Taken piano lessons, practised faithfully until she could play a wide range of classical pieces, and popular music for others to sing along to.

And she'd gone to modelling classes, learning the latest techniques for hair and make-up, how to stand and pose attractively, as well as how to inter-view and answer the faux-personal questions dur-ing her video confessionals.

Even rehearsed the likely screening questions until they were second nature, it was all right there in her head; she was as prepared as she could be.

She'd invested in waxing and a spray tan, a manicure and pedicure, even taken iontophoresis treatments to manage the nervous sweating for the duration of the contest.

That morning she'd done her hair and make-up and dressed in a neat, smooth black satin dress with just a hint of shine.

Her bag was packed with a swimsuit, a simple evening gown, and lightweight body armour.

Edina was as ready as she was ever going to be.

She smoothed the skirt of her dress down the length of a thigh.

Three months without the comfort and support of her family, and that room were difficult to con-template.

She took a deep breath and stood up.

It was time to leave.

Against her wishes, her family and friends were waiting in the lounge to say goodbye.

No one had said anything, but she felt her lips tremble, and tears gathering in her eyes.

"I wish you reconsider," her mother said.

She smiled a little, "I've worked too hard to get here."

"But hundreds of women from around the country will be there," her father said, "you'll never make it to the final ten."

"I have to try," she replied.

"I'm going to miss you so much," her best friend Sean said.

"Me too," and brushing a tear from her cheek, she dropped her bag and rushed across the room to hug him tightly.

"I have to go," she said, "before I start balling."

"Let me take you," he said.

Outside a car horn tooted, and she shook her head, "my taxi's here."

She hugged them all and left before they could try to change her mind again.

The crowd of people entering through the women's entrance of The Christmas Bonanza audi-tions at the hall was immense.

And when she saw the first of several crews filming the masses, she almost changed her mind and walked away.

Then she remembered what was at stake - she was here to prove herself. She was not going to let a mere billion women take it away.

Edina, you just have to take it minute by minute, she told herself, and squaring her shoulders, joined the sign in throng.

Getting signed in seemed the first challenge.

A long queue snaked down a series of corridors like a labyrinth.

She looked around while she waited, and no-ticed several cameras fixed to the walls and ceiling and nodded. Of course, it would be impossible to use a film crew in this crush. A sensible precau-tion.

She counted them as she went, and wondered if they were using facial recognition.

When she finally reached the head of the queue, she was waved through to one of several counters.

When she got to the counter, the young wom-an wearing a The Christmas Bonanza t-shirt behind it flipped through an enormous book and crossed her name off, and took a quick headshot.

Then printed it onto a luggage tag, fixed it to Edina's bag and dropped it on the conveyor belt behind her, saying, "your bag will be delivered to your destination."

Then she printed a name tag, an entry form, the Release of Liability waiver, and a sheaf of papers describing the competition terms and conditions.

Edina noted a camera fixed in such a way it was looking directly at her, and did not kid herself this was anything other than the first personality test.

She stood with poise, applied her name tag as soon as it was passed over, and chatted politely while she waited to complete the formalities.

When she was waved through to the next stage, she smiled, bowed a little, and thanked the woman for her time.

The first thing she saw was as she entered the next room was another camera, and then a woman in a black suit. She gave Edina a brief explanation of the terms, paying particular attention to the Re-lease of Liability.

In this instance, the camera was probably for due diligence, but she had no idea who was watch-ing.

She sat elegantly, asked intelligent questions about the details, and politely thanked the woman as she witnessed her signature on the forms.

She waved Edina through another door, where she joined another camera surveilled queue and was directed to a room where rows of desks were lined up like an examination hall.

Criss-crossed by camera angles.

A large digital display hanging on the wall at the front was set to 60:00.

When the desks were full, the door closed, and presumably, the queue moved onto the next room.

Several young women in tiny shorts and The Christmas Bonanza t-shirts started handing out quiz booklets labelled DO NOT TURN OVER UNTIL INSTRUCTED, along with multiple choice answer sheets 300 questions long and a lead pencil.

Another explained, "we're about to administer the first test, those of you who do not pass will be going home."

She disregarded the sound of anxious voices.

"You have one hour to complete 300 questions. The test is computer-graded, so please carefully colour in the circles."

She also disregarded the sound of someone fur-ther down retching.

"Your time starts now," she slapped a button on the desk starting the digital timer, "please turn over your question books."

The initial questions were easy enough, but by 15 minutes in, she was struggling and starting to tense up.

She took a deep breath and held it as she watched the clock tick over ten seconds before let-ting it out.

She reasoned the level of difficulty of the ques-tions would be random in an attempt to cull the numbers as much as possible.

Therefore, if she skimmed over the questions she couldn't immediately answer, she would an-swer more overall.

And once she'd gone through, she could go back and try the hard ones again.

She attempted to turn the pages quietly so the competition wouldn't catch what she was doing.

And by the time the clock signalled the end of the session, Edina had not only been proved cor-rect, but felt she'd answered way more questions than otherwise.

She permitted herself to stretch her arms and legs out as the women collected up the books, pencils, and answer sheets.

"Congratulations to you all.

"If you follow the corridor to the end, you'll find the dining hall where we've prepared a delicious lunch for you.

Toilet facilities are located on either side. You will be told where to go when lunch is over."

Chairs scraped on the floor as the competitors leapt to their feet to rush from the room, either to get the free food before it ran out, or the toilets.

Like disembarking plane passengers, clogging the corridor in the process.

Edina stayed seated until the stampede had moved on, then stood and pushed her chair back under the table. She thanked the women as she left the room.

What she really wanted to do, was run around to release some of the tension she'd built up during the test.

But with no mention of the outside, she settled for arm stretches as she walked up the corridor.

Having waited in the room, a toilet was free when she got there.

It was becoming a game as she checked for cameras, but there were none in the bathroom.

And having gone to the toilet first, dining room servers in the same tiny shorts and The Christmas Bonanza t-shirts were replenishing the buffet of hot and cold, sweet and savoury food.

She noted six cameras as she considered what the next event might be.

Most likely not napping.

Having just completed a quiz, probably not brain-related. Most likely something physical.

So, what she needed was something to provide a lot of energy, fight fatigue and keep hunger at bay for several hours of intense activity.

Probably not pizza, pasta, or burgers. Or the sugary and alcoholic drinks. Or the cakes and cookies.

Perhaps a piece of grilled chicken, and a baked potato with a light salad. Orange juice to drink. Followed by a banana or pear.

Taking just enough for her needs, to stop eating when she was about 80% full.

A woman in the service area caught her eye, and she smiled and nodded her thanks.

She found an empty seat, said hello to the women who were already there, and listened as they talked amongst themselves.

They clearly already knew each other and didn't think it was worth getting to know her. Mind you, none of them knew who would be progressing to the next stage anyway.

About an hour later, another woman in shorts and a sloganed t-shirt made an announcement.

"You have been placed into groups of 50; the details are posted in the next room. Please note the number of the coach you 've been assigned to, and make your way to the vehicles waiting to take you to the next destination for the next challenge."

Once again, chairs scraped as people rushed to leave. Edina collected her lunch things together, hesitated a moment, then collected together her table mates abandoned dishes, and took them all to the clearly marked return chute.

Once again, she saw a woman behind her coun-ter and she smiled her thanks and nodded.

She took her time, visiting the bathroom, and washing her hands, and when she got to the next room, the crowd had thinned out.

She noted her coach number, and half hoped her lunch uncompanions wouldn't land places in her coach. Or the show for that matter, because sharing a dormitory with those self-absorbed women would probably have been a nightmare.

Then again, she had no idea how many people applied, or how many had to be excluded before they made it to the show.

The first few episodes were usually devoted to narrowing the number of candidates down to 100 men and 100 women, so she supposed the day was all about getting rid of the low hanging fruit.

Was it even possible they might get down to 100 women today?

She didn't see the women from lunch as she boarded the coach, nor did she know anyone.

Not surprising really, she hadn't told anyone she was entering, because she was a little embarrassed about having applied.

She thought she was too old and didn't want to have to explain why.

Too late, she wished she hadn't written it in the application. That she was afraid of being alone for the rest of her life. That she was bored and wanted to meet new people.

But she supposed someone was already using it to prepare the marketing information about her.

And someone else was using it to script encounters she might have with her competitors.

The city scenery made way for the suburbs, and after about half an hour, the coach pulled up at a sports stadium.

Looked like her surmise was correct; an afternoon of sporting events.

A woman in the ubiquitous shorts and t-shirt stood up to make an announcement, Edina thought she recognised her from the morning's testing.

This time she explained the afternoon's events.

"Congratulations on progressing to the next stage. This afternoon is all about Athletics.

"You can choose any one of five events to com-pete in. The events are Discus, High Jump, Long Jump, Shot Put, and 400m Sprints.

"When you exit the bus, please follow the guides into the stadium. We've provided sports clothes and shoes, so check the tables on your way in.

"As you enter the stadium, you'll see signs for the events; please assemble at the appropriate sign.

"Good luck with your chosen event."

And with that, she left the coach and walked through the entry of the stadium.

As Edina changed into the same skimpy shorts and The Christmas Bonanza t-shirt as the crew and assistants were wearing, Edith was a little uncom-fortable. She wouldn't usually wear anything that tight or brief.

She packed her black dress and shoes in the bag the sports gear came in, and affixed the name sticker she'd been issued with to it.

Edina decided to do the sprint. She was more of a 100m sprinter, but it's not like there were likely to be any professional runners in the competition.

This time, film crews were allocated to each sport, and because they were in a professional venue, there were overhead cameras suspended on wires across the stadium.

The sprints started with the usual basic compe-tition; eight girls running the track, those who placed, rested and waited for the next race.

Those who didn't were escorted from the field.

The months spent running had served Edina well. She paced herself and came in the top three every race until the last.

Edina, she told herself, you've already made it, you have nothing to prove. But just for fun, why not try to win this time?

She smiled and thought why not?

So she put her game face on and ran as fast as she could, and was a little surprised when she won.

Even more surprised when they presented bronze, gold, and silver medals to the finalists of each event, in front of the crowd of competitors.

Was that a way to make early enemies?

The origianl t-shirted woman made another announcement, "Congratulations to the winners, and to you all.

"We've prepared an evening meal for you.

"But first you will be escorted to the change rooms where you can shower. Once more there are packs of clothes, shoes and toiletries to change into, so check in at the tables on your way in to claim your size.

"Your groups of fifty have been redistributed for the next leg; the details will be posted as you exit the change rooms.

"Please note your coach number, and look for the signs when you make your exit.

"You have thirty minutes to get ready."

Which triggered a rush to the clothing table.

Edina turned to congratulate her fellow finalists, "congratulations on your medal," she said, holding out her hand.

The silver medallist frowned, "do you think there'll be hair-dryers?"

"Probably not with only thirty minutes to pre-pare," Edina said.

"Shame, my hair frizzes when it's wet," said Bronze.

"Would you like to borrow my hair elastic to pull it back into a bun?" Edina asked.

"Actually, that would be great."

Edina pulled it off, dragged a few stray hairs from it, and handed it over.

"I have some bobby pins," silver offered.

Bronze smiled, "thank you. "My name's Joanna by the way."

"Bethany," said silver.

"Edina, pleased to meet you." She indicated the table where the crowd was thinning out, "shall we?"

They sauntered over, and Edina gestured for them to go first.

When Edina got to the table, they were out of her size, a size larger, and the size larger than that.

She smiled and shrugged, "can't be helped. I'll manage something," and taking the package, she followed what was left of the crowd to the shower room.

At least the shoes fit; white ballet style pumps with an elasticated type of fabric upper.

The dress was a plain, A-line white shift, with nothing to distinguish itself.

She hung it up and thought about her options while she was showered.

Was there anything she could use as a belt? Or a safety pin to fold it around her body in a faux-wrap dress? Or tie a knot in it?

She slathered on the generic moisturiser, put on the surprisingly stretchy undies, and aban-doned the bra.

There was no make-up included, which she im-agined would terrify some of the other competi-tors.

Luckily, she was one of the last in the room, and scouting around, found a couple of safety pins and an abandoned thin, blue ribbon on the floor. She towelled the ribbon dry, and hung it on a hook while she prepare to dress.

First she pinned up the dress's armholes. The slipped it on, folded the excess material across her front, and then tied the ribbon around her body, under her bust to hold the folds in place.

Not the best, not the worst, but it'd have to do.

She hurried out to meet the coach.

On the way, she wondered why everyone was wearing the same thing.

Her first thought was some kind of creepy vir-gin sacrifice, but the news had been covering the build-up to the competition.

Then she imagined the potentially amusing ex-planation of the mass slaughter to the police.

Which had never been the subject of news cov-erage in previous years.

And then more realistically, that they would be judging the female form.

Without any fancy clothes, make-up or elabo-rate hairstyles to distract them, they would be able to see the "real" girl.

Dusk was drawing in when they arrived at their destination; a large, Renaissance Revival style man-sion with a large tower positioned between two symmetrical wings.

Their destination was a large reception room on the ground floor of the tower. It had wooden floors and high ceilings of elaborately moulded and painted plaster.

That there were cameras in the corners came as no real surprise.

Large archways led to other rooms, presumably one of them being a dining room.

A grand piano sat in one corner, the stool slightly pulled out, as if the pianist had just nipped out for a quick ciggy.

At least three film crews were in attendance, and t-shirted people walked around offering half-full champagne glasses.

Edina was starting to get a little tired of seeing The Christmas Bonanza logo.

The women wearing the t-shirts all looked the same; same tiny shorts, the canvas sneakers, same sleek ponytails.

And seeing as they weren't offering anything else to drink, she took a glass of champagne, idly wondering how many women were in the room.

She looked around, trying to guess, and realised there weren't any men.

And considering further, she hadn't seen any men at any point since she'd walked into the audi-tion that morning.

Not entirely sure why that struck her as odd, as if they were a large harem attended only by wom-en.

It could just be a little something extra for the female competitor's comfort, but given the supposed cut-throat nature of the competition, it seemed counter to the spirit.

She sipped her champagne, and noticing Beth-any in the crowd, sent her a toast. She smiled and walked over.

"It's really quite beautiful here, isn't it?" she said.

Edina grunted agreement, "but all those Christmas Bonanza women are kinda creeping me out."

"Are they?" Bethany looked around her. "Now that I'm looking, they are kind of... I don't know, plasticky?" She took a sip of her champagne, "oh look, there's Joanna."

Bethany waved a hand to attract Joanna's atten-tion; her face brightened as she recognised them, and she walked across the room to them.

"Hello again," she said, smoothing back her hair, "thanks again for the elastic and hairpins - you're lifesavers."

Edina smiled and nodded, Bethany said, "you're welcome."

"Is it just me, or is there something about this place that strikes you as a bit odd?" Joanna asked.

"Edina was just saying about the women from the show."

"What about them?" Joanna looked at Edina

But she was looking at one in particular, "I could have sworn that was one of the women who shared my lunch table, but why would she be serv-ing here?"

Bethany and Joanna turned to watch as Edina approached the woman.

"Hello," she said to the woman, who attempted to brush past her, but Edina blocked her path, "Hello again."

The woman looked at her with no sign of recognition, and Edina took a step back, eyes wid-ening.

"What happened?" Bethany asked.

"There's no one there; her eyes are dead inside."

Bethany and Joanna exchanged a look.

"Okay then. We need to find someone else we know to check," Bethany said, and they looked ar-eound the room.

"Hold up," said Joanna, and approached anoth-er woman while Bethany and Edina watched.

Not long later she was back, "I knew her in high school, but she barely looked at me, and when I refused another glass, she just walked away!"

"Third time's the charm," Bethany said, crossing to another woman.

Then coming back, "I think we can safely say something is very wrong here."

They nodded, and Joanna asked, "but what?"

Edina rubbed her temple with one hand, then took a sip of her drink. "Is it possible the screening is not to get into the show, but whether you have the right kind of disposition to get sidelined into some other kind of activity?"

"Like a cult or something?" asked Bethany.

Joanna nodded, "I read something in the news about how runaways always spike this time of year, and no one knows why."

"No one would think to link it to The Christmas Bonanza auditions would they?" Bethany shivered.

Edina slapped her forehead, "and like big numpties, we walked in here willingly, leaving our friends and family thinking we'd be gone for three months, and all our worldly goods in the care of whoever these people are."

"I can't believe I did that. Not to mention sign-ing the non-disclosure agreement and liability waivers," Joanna said.

Bethany drummed her fingers on a thigh, "so, do we bail right now, or wait for... I don't know what."

"I feel like now might be best," Edina said, "be-fore they herd us back into the coaches to go to wherever our next destination is. Then again, this place is like a gussied-up prison, so it could well be the last stop."

"But how?" Joanna took a large gulp of her drink, "it's not like we can just walk out of here. And in any case, we have no idea where we are."

"Perhaps we should try to find a phone to call the police?" said Bethany.

"I was going to say, let's give ourselves an hour to find a phone and then go, but we don't have any way to tell the time either." Edina was starting to feel defeated.

They looked at each other miserably.

Edina stamped her foot. "I came here deter-mined to win this bloody thing, and now they've changed the rules. I am not going to lose to them.

"I don't think we can rely on anyone or any-thing except ourselves. We have to get out of this place, and the sooner the better. And if I have to walk/run, then I'm going to do just that."

The others looked at her doubtfully.

"I'm scared," Bethany said, and Joanna nodded.

"I understand. I don't know if I'm overreacting, and I don't know if I'm going to make it. But this time, I'm going to trust—"

They heard a crash as someone dropped a glass, and turned to look.

One of the younger competitors had dropped her glass and fainted.

"Just a little too much to drink," one of the show women said, as another couple of women clustered around her to help lift her up and carry her away.

Edina, Bethany and Joanna looked at each oth-er and found places to leave their half-empty glass-es.

As one they turned and started walking towards the entrance.

A show woman intercepted them, "where are you going?"

"Oh," said Edina, "just need the bathroom."

The woman looked suspicious, but directed them, "to your left as you go down the corridor."

"Thank you so much," said Bethany.

Joanna offered a bright smile, "lovely party."

Together they walked in the indicated direction, conscious of the woman looking after them.

"That was close," Joanna giggled nervously, "but I really do have to go now."

Edina splashed cold water on her face, then used the toilet.

Bathroom break taken care of, Edina opened the door a crack, "doesn't seem to be anyone watching," she whispered, "let's check any vehicles we see, and if we can't use them, we'll run for it, okay?"

The others nodded.

They managed to sneak out without anyone catching them.

Though with the number of cameras about, Edina couldn't be certain.

Crouching low, she ran to the first car she saw and tried the door.

It was locked! She ran on to the next.

Bethany ran to another, and got the door open, but couldn't find a key.

Joanna whistled, and having got their attention, she beckoned them over. The girls, crouching low, ran to the car and climbed inside.

"Fingers crossed," Joanna said, and turned the key.

It caught, and she gunned it, spraying gravel as she fishtailed up the long drive.

"Left or right?" she asked as she got to the end.

"Right," said Edina, the coach turned left to get into the place.

They drove for a few minutes, "wait, isn't this the Princess Freeway?" asked Bethany.

"I dunno, is it?" Joanna said, "and are we going in the right direction?"

They looked out into the darkness trying to tell.

"Hold up," Edina shouted, and Joanna slammed on the brakes, "I think we just passed a police sign."

Joanna grunted, "probably be repeated closer to the next junction," but she drove at something more closely approximating the speed limit.

After a few more kilometres, they followed the police signs through smaller and smaller streets until they reached the building.

Joanna pulled over and parked the car; "I have to admit I feel a little silly right now," she said.

"Me too," admitted Bethany.

"Me three," said Edina, "but if there's the small-est chance I'm right about the situation, I have to say something."

She got out of the car, and the others followed her into the police station.

And sat with her as she explained her gut feel-ing to a stony-faced detective.

Who said nothing for the longest time as he looked at her.

And then sighed.

"I'll send a car to investigate. In the meantime, you can call someone to come get you.

«« • »»

The scandal broke not long after.

That the Eternal Light Movement had created The Christmas Bonanza as a recruitment drive.

That almost all the competitors were brainwashed and sent away as slave labour within the first week.

That the footage of the first week was cut and pasted together into enough different episodes to last the full three months of programmed episodes.

That many of the sponsors had ties to the movement and benefited from the labourers.

That deprogrammers had been called in.

The tax office was investigating, along with other State and national regulatory bodies.

That three plucky competitors had been suspi-cious and led to the investigation that brought the movement down.

Closer to Christmas, Edina met up with Joanna and Bethany at a wine bar in the city.

They were shown to a booth, ordered some snacks and cocktails while they decided what to eat.

"I like how reassuringly normal this place is," commented Joanna.

"Oh yes," Bethany agreed.

Edina raised her glass, "to normality," and the others chinked glasses with her.

Bethany laid a hand on Edina's arm, "we had a lucky escape thanks to you."

Edina shrugged, "we did it together."

"I doubt I would've had the courage on my own," Joanna said.

Edina sipped her drink, "we were lucky; I shud-der to think what might have happened."

"So what's next?" asked Bethany, "I've got a new job."

Joanna grinned, "Nice one! I've applied to go to University."

They looked at Edina.

"I don't know. I'd pinned all my hopes on win-ning the competition for some kind of direction, and now that's gone. I think I need some time to grieve and let it go."

Bethany smoothed a lock of hair back behind her ears, "I understand, but don't take too long."

"Uh-huh," said Joanna, "think about the skills you didn't know you had. The ones that helped you see something wasn't quite right about the show.

"Why not put them to good use, like a journal-ist, perhaps the police force, or one of the agen-cies?"

Edina grunted, and speared some fried hal-loumi, "not sure I'd want to be in front of it again, but I could do some kind of analysis I guess."

She brightened, "something to think about an-yway."

She raised her glass again, "here's to a Merry Christmas, and an uneventful New Year."

Bethany raised her glass, "Merry Christmas."

"Definitely an uneventful New Year," agreed Jo-anna.

THE END

ABOUT THE AUTHOR

Alexandria Blaelock writes stories, some of them for *Ellery Queen's Mystery Magazine* and *Pulphouse Fiction Magazine*. She's also written five self-help books applying business techniques to personal matters like getting dressed, cleaning house, and feeding your friends.

As a recovering Project Manager, she's probably too fond of sticking to plan. She lives in a forest because she enjoys birdsong, the scent of gum leaves and the sun on her face. When not telecommuting to parallel universes from her Melbourne based imagination, she watches K-dramas, talks to animals, and drinks Campari. At the same time.

Discover more at www.alexandriablaelock.com.

BOOKS BY
ALEXANDRIA BLAELOCK

SHORT STORY COLLECTIONS

The Histories of Hayward Hall
Lovelorn, Lovestruck and Love at First Sight
Common or Garden Variety Heroes
Case Files of the Wilkinson Detective Agency
Unavoidable Fates
Christmas Travesties

OTHER FICTION

That Love Nonsense

MS BLAELOCK'S BOOKS

Stress Free Dinner Parties
Signature Wardrobe Planning
Holistic Personal Finance
Minimally Viable Housekeeping
Planning a Life Worth Living

SELECTED SHORT STORIES

Alma's Grace
Balancing the Book
Carmelita Basingstoke
Fate in Your Hands
Kiss of Death
Lady of the Looking Glass
Life in the Security Directorate
Long Weekend in the Snow
Love in the Past Tense
Love in the Security Directorate
Morning Star, Evening Star, Superstar
Needy Bitch
Payton's Run
Phoenix Child
Secret Singer
Shining Star
Ship in a Bottle
Simone Says Hands in the Air
Special Relativity in Space
The Bygone Boyfriend
The Day the Schedule Broke
The Ghost Detectors
The Guardian's Vigil
The Mince Pie Mystery
The Mystery of the Master Suite
The Pseudonym's Bride
The Shadow Thieves
The Time-Space Paradox
Toy Soldiers